Zoo Ah-Choooo

by **PETER MANDEL**

illustrated by
ELWOOD SMITH

Holiday House / New York

HOLIDAY HOUSE is registered in the U.S. Patent and Trademark Office.
Printed and Bound in November 2011 at Tien Wah Press, Johor Bahru, Johor, Malaysia.
The text typeface is Postcard Regular.
Elwood Smith used an M200 Pelikan fountain pen with an M250 nib, India ink,
Pelikan transparent watercolors, Arches cold press watercolor paper,
and Photoshop to create the images in this book.
www.holidayhouse.com
First Edition
1 3 5 7 9 10 8 6 4 2

Library of Congress Cataloging-in-Publication Data
Mandel, Peter, 1957-
Zoo Ah-choooo / by Peter Mandel ; illustrated by Elwood Smith. — 1st ed.
p. cm.
Summary: On a sleepy Sunday at the zoo,
all the animals suddenly begin to sneeze.
ISBN 978-0-8234-2317-0 (hardcover)
[1. Zoo animals—Fiction. 2. Zoos—Fiction. 3. Sneezing—Fiction.]
I. Smith, Elwood H., 1941- ill. II. Title.
PZ7.M31223Zo 2011
[E]—dc22
2010029434

For Lois,
an animal person
if ever there was one
P. M

To Maggie,
my wife and creative partner
E. S.

It was a sleepy Sunday at the City Zoo.
The Hippos were slow. Low and slow.

The Sloth was asleep. Deeply asleep.
Even the Seals swam slowly.
It was a slow zoo show.

Suddenly, something unsleepy—a long, LOUD SOUND—flew through the zoo!

It was a Zoo Ah-chooOO.

Where did it come from? From the Snow Leopard.
What did he do? He went Ah-chooOO!
It was a Leopard's sneeze.
Just one.

But the African Elephant heard the sound.
She raised her trunk...
RRRrrr-eeeEEE-ahh-

PHOOOO!!!
Elephant sneeze. Stand back.

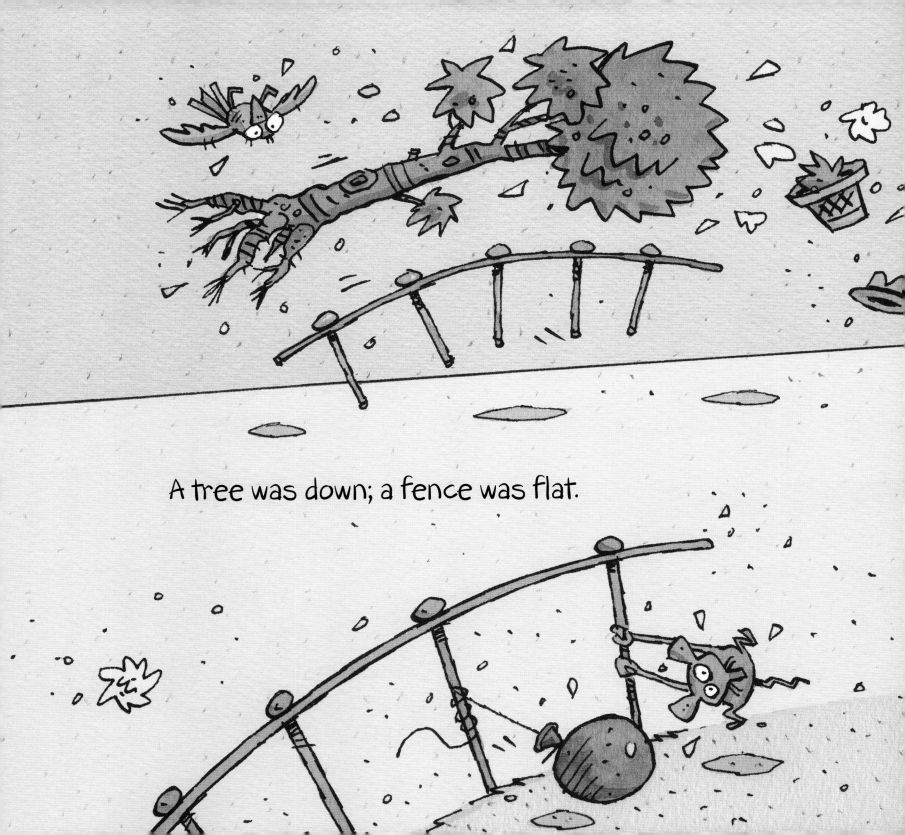

A tree was down; a fence was flat.

The Zoo Ah-chooOO was catching.
The Hippo in his mud bath
felt a tickle in his nose.

Kahaaaaaaa...

The Zookeeper came running with nose drops and a giant tissue. Too late.

Kah-*bah*-RUMpppphhhHHHH!!!
The Hippo's sneeze erupted.

It made a MUD volcano.
"Oh, no!" cried the Zookeeper.

Mud was covering the animals.
"Is that a chocolate giraffe?"
said a visitor.

But then the mud began to crack:
Wah-heeEEE-ahh-raaaaaAAAK!!!
sneezed the Giraffe.

Chunks of chocolaty gunk rained down everywhere. People put up umbrellas.

The Zookeeper tried wiping Zebras
with spray cleaner.

Even the Sloth woke up and found his washcloth to scrub.

The Seals sudsed and rinsed. The zoo was hard at work until . . .

at once, the whiskers
on every single Seal felt tickly.

Ahh-ahhhh-ahhhhh . . .

Ka-FrrroooOOOOOOOOMMMMM!!!

It was a Twelve-Seal Sneeze.
All twelve zoo Seals. At once!

The Seal pond splashed up high like
a gusher, gushing rings and rubber balls.
"Is that Old Faithful?" said a visitor.

The Zookeeper knew he had
to act. Act fast.
Flamingos were floating.

Foxes were fishing.
The Polar Bear hung on to his iceberg.
It was not a slow zoo day at all!

The Zookeeper got the
African Elephant to refill the Seal pond.
Then he called the Large-Animal Vet.

What did the Animal Doctor do?
He made every zoo animal drink
a SUPERFIZZY sneeze solution.

"Is that root beer?" said a visitor.
It was FIZZY sneeze solution.
No more Zoo Ah-chooOO.

It was the Snow Leopard.
Definitely not a sneeze.
And not a burp.
A Leopard's
YAWN.
Just one.
(But it might
be catching.)
Did anyone hear it?
Did the Elephant?
Did the Hippo
in his mud bath?
Did you?